D1639382

Father Christmas Letters

J.R.R. TOLKIEN

Father Christmas Letters

HarperCollins*Publishers*

Father Christmas Letters

*Every year the children of J.R.R. Tolkien
received a letter from Father Christmas.
In it he described the hilarous events
that took place at the North Pole during
the preparations for his annual visit. Most
of the disasters were caused by Father
Christmas's chief assistant, the North
Polar Bear, whose insatiable curiosity and
sense of fun were responsible for many of
the mishaps.*

*Later Father Christmas took on as his
secretary an Elf named Ilbereth who took*

to writing letters himself when Father Christmas was too busy.

This miniature book contains only a selection of the letters written over a period of 20 years through the childhoods of J.R.R. Tolkien's four children. Sometimes the envelopes, dusted with snow and bearing Polar postage stamps, were found in the house; sometimes the postman brought them; and letters that the children wrote themselves vanished from the fireplace when no one was about. But whatever the circumstances, from 1920 to 1939 no year passed without a letter.

Christmas House
NORTH POLE
1920

Love to
daddy, mummy
michael g aunt e
& mary

Dear John,

I heard you ask daddy
what I was like & where
I lived. I have drawn
ME & My House for you.
Take care of the picture.
I am just off now for
Oxford with my bundle
of toys — some for you.
Hope I shall arrive in
time: the snow is very
thick at the NORTH POLE
tonight. Yr loving Fr. Chr.

1920

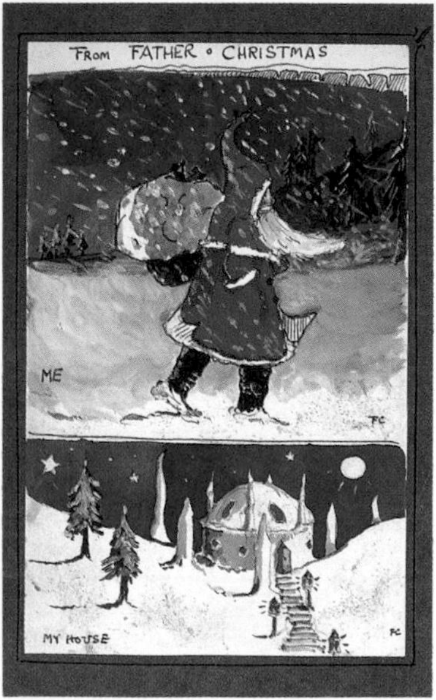
FROM FATHER CHRISTMAS
ME
FC
MY HOUSE
FC

Christmas House
North Pole

1920
Love to Daddy, Mummy, Michael
and Auntie Mary

Dear John

I heard you ask daddy what I was
like and where I lived. I have drawn
ME & My House for you. Take care
of the picture. I am just off now for
Oxford with my bundle of toys –
some for you. Hope I shall arrive
in time: the snow is very thick at the
NORTH POLE tonight:

Yr Loving Fr. Chr.

1925

I am dreadfully busy this year – it makes my hand more shaky than ever when I think of it – and not very rich. In fact, awful things have been happening, and some of the presents have got spoilt and I haven't got the North Polar Bear to help me and I have had to move house just before Christmas, so you can imagine what a state everything is in, and you will see why I have a new address. It all happened like this: one very windy day last November my hood blew off and went and stuck on the top of the North

Pole. I told him not to, but the North Polar Bear climbed up to the thin top to get it down – and he did. The pole broke in the middle and fell on the roof of my house, and the North Polar Bear fell through the hole it made into the dining room with my hood

over his nose, and all the snow fell off
the roof into the house and melted and
put out all the fires and ran down into
the cellars where I was collecting this
year's presents, and the North Polar
Bear's leg got broken. He is well again
now, but I was so cross with him that

he says he won't try to help me again. I
expect his temper is hurt, and will be
mended by next Christmas. I send you
a picture of the accident, and of my
new house on the cliff above the North
Pole (with beautiful cellars in the cliffs).

1926

I am more shaky than usual this year.
The North Polar Bear's fault! It was the
biggest bang in the world, and the most
monstrous firework there ever has
been. It turned the North Pole BLACK
and shook all the stars out of place,
broke the moon into four – and the
Man in it fell into my back garden. He
ate quite a lot of my Christmas
chocolates before he said he felt better,

and climbed back to mend it and get
the stars tidy. Then I found out that the
reindeer had broken loose. They were
running all over the country, breaking
reins and ropes and tossing presents up
in the air. They were all packed up to
start, you see – yes it only happened

this morning; it was a sleighload of
chocolate things – which I always send
to England early. I hope yours are not
badly damaged. But isn't the North
Polar Bear silly? And he isn't a bit
sorry! Of course he did it – you
remember I had to move last year

because of him? The tap turning on the Aurora Borealis fireworks is still in the cellar of my old house. The North Polaṛ Bear knew he must never, never touch it. I only let it off on special days like Christmas. He says he thought it was cut off since we moved – anyway he was nosing round the ruins this morning soon after breakfast (he hides things to eat there) and turned on all the Northern Lights for two years in one go. You have never heard or seen anything like it. I have tried to draw a picture of it; but I am too shaky to do it properly and you can't paint fizzing light, can you?

Love from Father Christmas
1926.

1927

It has been so bitter at the North Pole lately that the North Polar Bear has spent most of the time asleep and has been less use this Christmas. The North Pole became colder than any cold thing ever has been, and when the North Polar Bear put his nose against it, it took the skin off: that is why it is bandaged with red flannel in the picture (but the bandage has

slipped). Why did he? I don't know,
but he is always putting his nose where
it oughtn't to be – into my cupboards,
for instance.

Also it has been very dark here since
winter began. We haven't seen the Sun,
of course, for three months, and there
are no Northern Lights this year – you
remember the awful accident last year?

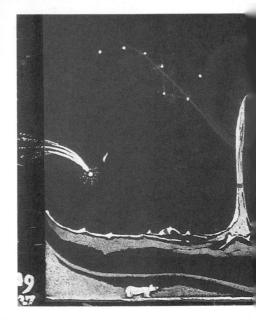

There will be none again until the end
of 1928. The North Polar Bear has got
his cousin (and distant friend), the
GREAT BEAR, to shine extra bright
for us, and this week I have hired a
comet to do my packing by, but it

doesn't work as well – you can see that by my picture. The North Polar Bear has not really been any more sensible this year: yesterday he was snowballing the Snow-man in the garden and pushed him over the edge of the cliff so that he fell into my sleigh at the bottom and broke lots of things– one of them was himself. I used some of what was left of him to paint my white picture.

Father Christmas

"Top o' the World"

NORTH POLE

Thursday December 20th

1928

1928

What do you think the poor dear old bear has been and done this time? Nothing as bad as letting off all the lights. Only fell from top to bottom of the main stairs on Thursday! We were beginning to get the first lot of parcels down out of the store-rooms into the hall. Polar Bear would insist on taking an enormous pile on his head as well as lots in his arms. Bang Rumble Clatter Crash! awful moanings and growlings:

I ran out onto the landing and saw he
had fallen from top to bottom onto his
nose leaving a trail of balls bundles
parcels and things all the way down –
and he had fallen on top of some and
smashed them. I hope you got none of
these by accident? I have drawn you a
picture of it all. Polar bear was rather
grumpy at my drawing it: he says my
Christmas pictures always make fun

of him and that one year he will send
you one drawn by himself of me being
idiotic (but of course I never am, and
he can't draw well enough). When he
had picked himself up he ran out of
doors and wouldn't help clear up
because I sat on the stairs and laughed
as soon as I found there was not much
damage done.

But anyway I thought you would like a picture of the INSIDE of my new big house for a change. This is the chief hall under the largest dome where we pile all the presents usually, ready to load the sleighs at the doors. Polar Bear and I built it nearly all ourselves, and laid all the blue and mauve tiles. The banisters and roof are not quite straight, but it doesn't really matter. I painted the pictures on the walls of the trees and stars and suns and moons.

1929

It is a light Christmas again, I am glad
to say – the Northern Lights have been
specially good. We had a bonfire this
year (to please the Polar Bear), to
celebrate the coming in of winter. The
Snow-elves let off all the rockets
together which surprised us both. I
have tried to draw you a picture of it,
but really there were hundreds of
rockets. You can't see the Elves at all
against the snow background. The

bonfire made a hole in the ice and woke
up the Great Seal, who happened to be
underneath. The Polar Bear let off

20,000 silver sparklers afterwards –
used up all my stock, so that is why I
had none to send you. Then he went

for a holiday!!! – to north Norway –
and stayed with a wood-cutter called
Olaf, and came back with his paw all
bandaged just at the beginning of our
busy times.

There seem more children than ever in
all the countries I specially look after. It
is a good thing clocks don't tell the
same time all over the world or I
should never get round, although when

my magic is strongest – at Christmas – I
can do about a thousand stockings a
minute, if I have it all planned out
beforehand. You could hardly guess the
enormous piles of lists I make out. I
seldom get them mixed. But I am rather
worried this year. You can guess from
my pictures what happened. The first
one shows you my office and packing
room and the Polar Bear reading out
names while I copy them down. We

had awful gales here, worse than you
did, tearing clouds of snow to a million
tatters, screaming like demons, burying
my house almost up to the roofs. Just
at the worst the Polar Bear said it was

stuffy! and opened a north window before I could stop him. Look at the result – only actually the North Polar Bear was buried in papers and lists; but that did not stop him laughing.

1930

I have enjoyed all your letters: I hope
you will like your stockings this year: I
tried to find what you asked for, but the
stores have been in rather a muddle –
you see the Polar Bear has been ill. He
had whooping-cough first of all. I could
not let him help with the packing and
sorting which begins in November –
because it would be simply awful if any
of my children caught Polar Whooping

Cough and barked like bears on Boxing
Day. So I had to do everything myself
in the preparations. Of course Polar
Bear has done his best – he cleaned up
and mended my sleigh and looked after
the reindeer while I was busy. That is
how the really bad accident happened.
Early this month we had a most awful
snow-storm (nearly six feet of snow)
followed by an awful fog. The poor

Polar Bear went out to the reindeer
stable and got lost and nearly buried. I
did not miss him or go to look for him
for a long while. His chest had not got
well from Whooping Cough so this
made him frightfully ill, and he was in
bed until three days ago. Everything
has gone wrong and there has been no
one to look after my messengers
properly. Aren't you glad the Polar

Bear is better? We had a party of Snow-
boys (sons of the Snow-men, which are
the only sort of people that live near –
not of course men *made* of snow,
though my gardener who is the oldest
of all the Snow-men sometimes draws a
picture of a *made* Snow-man instead of
writing his name) and Polar Cubs (the
Polar Bear's nephews) on Saturday, as
soon as he felt well enough. He didn't

Party of Snowboys & Pol

...cubs to celebrate P. B.'s recovery.

eat much tea, but when the big cracker
went off after, he threw away his rug,
and leaped in the air, and has been well
ever since.

The first picture shows Polar Bear
telling a story after all the things had

been cleared away. The little pictures
show me finding Polar Bear in the
snow, and Polar Bear sitting with his
feet in hot mustard and water to stop
him shivering. It didn't – and he
sneezed so terribly he blew five candles
out. Still, he is all right now – I know

covers!

because he has been at his tricks again: quarrelling with the Snow-man (my gardener) and pushing him through the roof of his snow house; and packing lumps of ice instead of presents in naughty children's parcels. That might be a good idea only he never told me and some of them (with ice) were put in

warm store-rooms and melted all over good children's presents! Well, my dears, there is lots more I should like to say – about my Green Brother, and my father, old Grandfather Yule, and why we were both called Nicholas after the Saint (whose day is December sixth) who used to give secret presents,

sometimes throwing purses of money
through the window. But I must hurry
away – I am late already and I am
afraid you may not get this in time.

1937

By
Elf
Messenger

I am afraid I have not had any time to
draw you a picture this year. You see
I strained my hand moving heavy
boxes in the cellars in November and
could not start my letters until later
than usual and my hand still gets tired
quickly. But Ilbereth, who is now my
secretary, has done you what he calls
a picture diary. I hope it will do.

Dear children,

Shall I tell you about my pictures?
Polar Bear and Valkotukka and Paksu
are always lazy after Christmas, or
rather after the St Stephen's Day Party.
Father Christmas is ringing for
breakfast in vain.

Nobody wants breakfast *after*
Christmas. N̂B̂ P̂. and V̂ are tired
1926.   (and full).

Another day when Polar Bear as
usual was late, Paksu threw a bath-
sponge full of icy water on his face.
Polar Bear chased him all round
the house and round the garden
and then forgave him, because he
had not caught Paksu, but had
found a huge appetite.

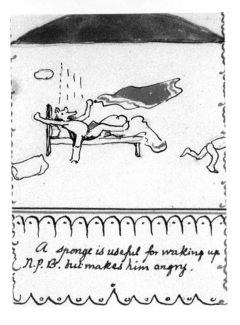

A sponge is useful for waking up N.P.B. but makes him angry.

We had terrible weather at the end of winter, and actually had rain. We could not go out for days. I have drawn Polar Bear and his nephews when they did venture out.

Late Spring 1937. Thaw and rain.
Going for a nice walk to find a lost
appetite.

Paksu and Valkotukka have never gone away. They like it so much that they have begged to stay. It was much too warm at the North Pole this year. A large lake formed at the bottom of the cliff, and left the North Pole standing on an island. I have drawn a view looking South so the cliff is on the other side. It was about midsummer.

Midsummer. Great hole appears in ice. Seals come out. NPB takes to boating.

*The North Polar Bear took to trying
to paddle a boat or canoe, but he fell
in so often that the seals thought he
liked it, and used to get under the boat
and tip it up. That made him annoyed.
The sport did not last long as the water
froze again early in August.*

Then we began to begin to think of this Christmas. In my picture, Father Christmas is dividing up the lists and giving me my special lot – you are in it. North Polar Bear of course always pretends to be managing everything: that is why he is pointing, but I am really listening to Father Christmas and I am saluting him, not North Polar Bear.

Beginning to think of next Christmas. Ilbereth getting orders from F.C.

We had a glorious bonfire and fireworks to celebrate the Coming of Winter, and the beginning of real 'Preparations'.

Celebrating the Coming of Winter.
Bonfire party and fireworks.

The snow came down very thick in November and the Elves and Snow-boys had several toboganning half-holidays. The Polar Cubs were not good at it. They fell off, and most of them took to rolling or sliding down just on themselves.

Tobogganing down from Cliff House. Snowboys have a good time

Today – but this is the best bit: I had just finished my picture, or I might have drawn it differently. Polar Bear was being allowed to decorate a big tree in the garden, all by himself and a ladder.

Today, Dec. 23rd. NPB busy
with the tree — before the disaster

*Suddenly we heard terrible growly-squealy noises. We rushed out to find Polar Bear hanging in the tree himself! 'You are **not** a decoration,' said Father Christmas. 'Anyway, I am alight,' he shouted. He was. We threw a bucket of water over him, which spoilt a lot of the decorations, but saved his fur. The silly old thing had rested the ladder against a branch (instead of the trunk of the tree). Then he thought,*

'I will just light the candles to see if they are working,' although he was told not to. So he climbed to the tip of the ladder with a taper. Just then the branch cracked, the ladder slipped on the snow, and Polar Bear fell into the tree and caught on some wire, and his fur got caught on fire. Luckily he was rather damp, or he might have fizzled. I wonder if roast Polar is good to eat?

The last picture is imaginary, and not very good. But I hope it will come true. It will if Polar Bear behaves. I hope you can read my writing. I try to write like dear old Father Christmas

Tomorrow. Starting with
the first load.

(2|b)

*(without the trembles), but I cannot do
so well. I can write Elvish better:*

*That is some – but Father Christmas
says I write even that too spidery and
you would never read it; it says:*
A VERY MERRY CHRISTMAS TO YOU ALL.

Love, Ilbereth.

NORTH ✦✦✦ POLE
XT ✦✦✦✦✦ MAS
1937

Christopher & Priscilla
20 Northmoor Road
Oxford
England

A Merry Christmas 1937
F.C.

HarperCollins*Publishers*
77-85 Fulham Palace Road
Hammersmith, London W6 8JB

This one-volume miniature edition published 1998
9 8 7 6 5 4 3 2 1

The Father Christmas Letters edited by Baillie Tolkien
were first published by Allen & Unwin in 1976
Miniature edition first published as
3-volume set in 1994

Text and pictures copyright
© George Allen & Unwin (Publishers) Ltd 1976

ISBN 0 261 10369 5

🖋® is a registered trademark of
the J.R.R.Tolkien Estate Limited

Printed in Hong Kong

You can read more about Father
Christmas's adventures in the large-format
The Father Christmas Letters,
published by HarperCollins*Publishers*,
ISBN 0 261 10255 9.